In the Field

Written by Joanne L. S. Risso
Illustrated by Missi Allen

In the Field

Copyright © 2013, by Joanne L. S. Risso.
Cover Copyright ©, 2013 by Sunbury Press, Inc. and Missi Allen

NOTE: This is a work of fiction. Names, characters, places and incidents are the product of the author's imagination or are used fictitiously, and any resemblance to actual persons, living or dead, business establishments, events or locales is entirely coincidental.

All rights reserved, including the right to reproduce this book or portions thereof in any form whatsoever. For information contact Sunbury Press, Inc., Subsidiary Rights Dept., 50 W Main St., Mechanicsburg, PA 17055 USA or legal@sunburypress.com.

For information about special discounts for bulk purchases, please contact Sunbury Press, Inc. Wholesale Dept. at (855) 338-8359 or orders@sunburypress.com.

To request one of our authors for speaking engagements or book signings, please contact Sunbury Press, Inc. Publicity Dept. at publicity@sunburypress.com.

FIRST SUNBURY PRESS EDITION

Printed in the United States of America
June 2013

ISBN 978-1-62006-247-0

Published by:
Sunbury Press, Inc.
50 West Main Street
Mechanicsburg, PA   17055

www.sunburypress.com

Mechanicsburg, Pennsylvania   USA

To Ella's Warren,
Reading takes you places!
2014

For Pete:

Who digs and toils in the earth with hands bare and heart happy.

J.L.S.R.

One warm day in early spring, Manny went outside to play by the swings near his mother. After she pushed his little sister on the swing, she sat down on the bench and sighed. Manny looked at the farmer's fields. He picked up his red shovel and walked into the field, where the orange dandelions grew wild and tangled around his feet. He picked three flowers and carried them on his shovel back to the bench.

"I love you, Mom," Manny said, as he held out the shovel towards his mother.
"Thank you, Manny," she said, with a wide smile and a twinkle in her eyes. Then she looked out at the fields.

The next day Manny went outside to play by the swings near his mother. After she pushed his little sister on the swing, she sat down on the bench and sighed. Manny looked at the farmer's fields. He picked up his red bucket and walked into the field, where the pink clover grew wild and tangled around his feet. He filled his bucket with flowers and carried them back to the bench.

"I love you, Mom," Manny said, as he held out the bucket towards his mother.
"Thank you, Manny," she said, with a wide smile.
Then she looked out at the fields.

In summer, when the sun was high in the deep blue sky, Manny went outside to play by the swings near his mother. After she pushed his little sister on the swing, she sat down on the bench and sighed. Manny looked at the farmer's fields. He picked up the handle of his red wagon and pulled it behind him, into the fields where the yellow buttercups grew wild and tangled around his feet. He plucked and picked at the flowers until his wagon was full, and pulled it back to the bench.

"I love you, Mom," Manny said, as the wagon stopped at his mother's feet.
"Thank you, Manny," she said, with a smile. Then she looked out at the fields.

The next day Manny went outside to play by the swings near his mother. After she pushed his little sister on the swing, she sat down on the bench and sighed. Manny looked at the farmer's fields. He took hold of his father's red wheelbarrow and pushed it into the field, where the violet alfalfa grew wild and tangled around his feet. He pulled and tugged at the flowers until the wheelbarrow was full, and pushed the heavy laden barrow back to the bench.

"I love you, Mom," Manny said, as the wheelbarrow thudded to a halt at his mother's feet.
"Thank you, Manny," she said. Then she looked out at the fields.

Manny sat beside his mother on the bench, and looked out at the fields too. He looked for the dandelions, but he saw none. He looked for the clover, but he saw none. He looked for the buttercups, but he saw none. He looked for the alfalfa, but he saw none. Manny sighed.

One crisp, cool day in late fall, when the sun set early in the pearly sky, Manny sat on the bench. Where dandelions and clover, buttercups and alfalfa once grew, there was a vast expanse of dried out stems and protruding rocks scattered across the field. The encroaching patch of pumpkin vines, with a single pumpkin, left behind when the pickers passed, sat waiting to be carved.

The days grew cool and the nights grew long. Manny did not go outside much in the winter, when the sun hid weakly behind the clouds. His mother stayed inside. Sometimes she would sit by the window, and look out past the swings, into the field. Snow covered the ground and the chains on the swings were frozen. Cardinals, nuthatches and titmice flitted along the branches and hopped on the snow under the trees. They scratched and pecked, searching for seeds and insects. Manny's mother sighed. Manny watched his mother.

When March came blowing in, Manny's father gave him some packets of wildflower seeds. Manny went outside and filled his red bucket with water. He put his bucket in his red wagon and pulled it behind him, into the fields. He carefully laid seed after seed on the cold, hard ground. He dusted them with soil and sprinkled water on each one. Then Manny pulled his wagon home and went inside. He sat by the window and looked out past the swings, into the field.

The next day he sat by the window and waited. Gray clouds gathered overhead. Wind whistled through the cracks around the window. Rain splashed down and soaked into the ground. It dripped off the swing, and made a muddy pool under the bench. It rained on the hills. It rained on the fields. It rained on Manny's seeds.

When the days grew warm again, and spring began creeping across the land, Manny went outside to play by the swings near his mother. After she pushed his little sister on the swing, she sat down on the bench and sighed. Manny's mother looked out at the fields.

"I love you, Manny," she said, with a wide smile and a twinkle in her eyes. She put her arm around Manny's shoulders and gave him a squeeze.

"Thank you, Mom," said Manny, and he looked out at all the orange and pink and yellow and violet flowers growing wild and tangled in the field.

Field Notes

Dandelion: This flowering plant is a native to North America. Its botanical name is *Taraxacum officinale*. It grows most commonly as a weed and is entirely *edible*. This means people can eat it. It produces yellow or orange flowers which open during the day and close at night. When mature, the flower head looks like a white, hairy sphere. Hundreds of tiny 'parachutes' then blow off in the wind and scatter seeds.

Clover: This flowering plant is also known as trefoil and belongs to the pea family. Its botanical name is *Trifolium*, which means 'three leaves'. Often clover is grown as *fodder* for animals. It is nutritious for livestock. The flower heads are a whitish color, often tinged with pink or cream. They are often called 'shamrock' and are considered lucky if found with four leaves instead of three.

Buttercup: This flowering perennial has bright yellow or white flowers. Its botanical name is *Ranunculus*, which means 'little frog' in Latin. It is commonly used as food for many moths and butterflies. Buttercups are poisonous to cattle, horses and other livestock when eaten fresh. Buttercup flowers are very bright and shiny, and when held near skin will reflect a yellow light.

Alfalfa: This flowering plant belongs to the pea family. Its botanical name is *Medicago sativa L.* It is most commonly grown as a *forage* crop. This means it is grown for animals to eat. It can be cut three or four times per year, and harvested as hay or turned into silage. It looks like tall clover with small purple flowers. Alfalfa can grow up to 3 feet tall, and can live as long as 20 years.

Tufted Titmouse: These little gray birds from the *Paridae* Family, are commonly found in the Eastern United States. They have a lighter colored belly and tufted feathers on their heads. They are very acrobatic and can hang upside down to eat insects. They sound like they are singing "*Peter, Peter, Peter.*"

Nuthatch: The White-Breasted Nuthatch often flocks with titmice and chickadees. They are from the Family *Sittidae* and are tree-climbing birds that *glean* insects from the bark of trees. They have large heads, short tails, and short legs. They have a white breast, a black cap over their head, and blue-gray backs with black stripes across their wing feathers, and black and white stripes across their tail feathers.

Cardinal: The Northern Cardinal, from the *Cardinalidae* Family, mostly eats seeds. The male is a vibrant red color with a black mask on its face and a tuft on its head. The female is a reddish-gray color with a gray mask.

Bird photos © Kathy M. Miller www.celticsunrise.com

References

Richard H. Uva, Joseph C. Neal and Joseph M. Ditomaso, *Weeds of The Northeast*, (Ithaca, NY: Cornell University Press, 1997)

GRIN (Germplasm Resources Information Network) Taxonomy for Plants, www.ars-grin.gov

Encyclopedia Britannica, www.britannica.com

Invasive and Noxious Weeds, www.plants.usda.gov

Birds of Eastern United States, www.birdingguide.com

Birds of North America, St. Martin's Press, 2001.

Grow your own Garden

Whether you have a large back yard with rolling farm fields like 'Manny'; a small suburban lot with close neighbors; or an inner city apartment with no yard, growing your own garden is possible.

Plants need three main things; water, food and sunlight. They also need someone to care for them. Plants can be grown outside or inside, in plant pots or containers, or recycled containers from your house. Most plants need healthy soil that drains well. If you use a recycled container, punch holes in the bottom to let the water drain through, and rest the container in another shallow dish or plate.

You can buy seeds at stores, or collect them from flowers you find outside. You might try flowers or vegetables. Take special care of seeds when they start to grow. Remember to water them a little each day, but not too much. You don't want to drown them! Place your plants outside in the sun (in spring and summer), or on a sunny windowsill. You can also place a glass or plastic container (tipped upside down) over the top of the plants to provide more warmth.

For more information on growing your own plants, browse some of the following sites, or visit your local library and find books on gardening.

Growing Alfalfa Sprouts: www.backyardnature.net/simple/alf-spr.htm
Gardening for Kids: www.lucygardens.com
Indoor Gardens: www.humeseeds.com/kids.htm

Other Ways to Keep Flowers

Instead of picking all the beautiful flowers you see outdoors, try one of the following activities:

- Draw or sketch a picture.
- Take a photograph.
- Use acrylics or watercolors to paint a picture.
- Make your own flowers using colored paper.
- Make a bouquet using tissue paper petals.

Or try one of these Eco-Crafts:

- Cut flowers out of old fabric and glue onto paper.
- Recycle cereal boxes by cutting out large flower shapes and gluing plastic bottle caps onto the middle.
- Make yo-yo flowers by following these directions:
- Cut a circle about 4" in diameter, from fabric.
- Use a needle and thread (with a knot at one end) to make a running stitch about a quarter of an inch from the outside edge of the circle all the way around.
- Pull the end of the thread firmly to gather the edges of the circle in to the center and tie a knot to secure the thread.
- Neaten the fabric with your fingers, to make your flower flat and round.
- Glue the top of a popsicle stick or a twig from a dead tree, to the back of the flower. Display a bunch of flowers in a jar.

Photo by www.mitzismiscellany.com

Joanne L.S. Risso was born and raised in Gippsland, Australia. Trained as a teacher, she has worked with children deep in the heart of Africa, Asia, Europe, Australia and North America. Joanne and her family take care of their garden: full of vegetables and flowers and weeds! She lives with her husband and four children in Central Pennsylvania. Please visit www.joannerisso.com to learn more about the author.

Missi Brenneman-Allen lives peacefully and works happily in Schuylkill Haven, Pennsylvania. Please visit www.missiallenart.com to learn more about the artist.

Other books: *Over the Sea* by Joanne L.S. Risso, illustrated by Kathy Connelly, Sunbury Press, 2011.

CPSIA information can be obtained at www.ICGtesting.com
Printed in the USA
BVOW101345160613

323415BV00004B/10/P